September Blackberries

ALSO BY MICHAEL McCLURE

The Adept
The Beard
Dark Brown
Gargoyle Cartoons
Ghost Tantras
Hymns to St. Geryon
Little Odes
The Mad Cub
Meat Science Essays
The New Book / A Book of Torture
Passage
Star

September Blackberries

Michael McClure

A NEW DIRECTIONS BOOK

PS
3563
A262
S38
1974

3/1974
am. Lit

ACKNOWLEDGMENTS

Grateful acknowledgment is made to the editors and publishers of the various publications in which many of the poems in this book first appeared: *Bastard Angel, The Berkeley Barb, The Berkeley Tribe, Brittania, Café Solo, Clear Creek, Cranium Broadsides, Crawdaddy, The Daily Cal, Ginger, Green Flag, Kaleidoscope, Kayak, Mark in Time, Mojo Navigator, New Departures, New York Quarterly, Paris Review, Plane Poems, Poetry Review, Rolling Stone, Shantih, Show, Tansy/Wakarusa Broadsides, Unmuzzled Ox, Win, The World.*

The quote that begins the poem titled *For James B. Rector* is from *Anatomy of the Cell* by Bjorn Afzelius, Phoenix Science Series, University of Chicago Press.

Manufactured in the United States of America
First published clothbound (ISBN: 0–8112–0523–1) and as New Directions Paperbook 370 (ISBN: 0–8112–0524–x) in 1974
Published simultaneously in Canada by McClelland & Stewart, Ltd.

New Directions Books are published for James Laughlin
by New Directions Publishing Corporation,
333 Sixth Avenue, New York 10014

"Now I am in Arden—the more fool I . . ."
—*As You Like It*

FOREWORD

Each poem should be an experiment—in the sense that there are experiments in alchemy and biochemistry. I have my transient meatflesh to play on as if it is a harp. I see all beings as a finger or tentacle of a universe that is a surge of living matter. When I make a poem I create an extension of myself. I can feel more when I write a poem. A poem is like a nasturtium or a tiny orchid in a ponderosa pine forest. A poem is like a panda —or a giant ground sloth—or like the breath of a wolf on a frosty evening. A poem is an amino acid in the ripples of an endless sea.

A poem is like an ear or shoulder. Poetry is the way that we extend our inner life. The real inner life is cut off from us—but we can put it out there and call it a poem. We stand on poetry— like a steppingstone in a torrent—and are more free. Then we find the steppingstone is a drunken boat and we're sailing, whirling, laughing . . .

M. M.

WRITTEN ABOVE THE SIERRAS
IN THE FLYLEAF OF REGIS DEBRAY'S
REVOLUTION IN THE REVOLUTION

for Joanna

Shouldst thou die, I'll be with thee
in the mountains of eternity
and fight thy cause with gun and harp.
I am only paws
and claws within this mortal world.
The map
of silk and marble
BOW TO THEE.
I praise FUTURITY
within the forests
of the mind
MADE REAL.

Running. Breathing. Speaking.

Beating music with a feather.

1

FOR YOU

AHH—HERE IS MY MEAT LOVE! I HAVE BEEN
IN THE BLUE VALLEYS,
IN THE VISIONS OF UMBER
AND BEIGE AND GOLD!
—And dived through the universes of old
addictions to image and word.

HERE I AM—AGAIN!
With my heart in my hand.
Proportionless I stand,
in vibrations of things and Matter.
Only skin can shatter
the meaningless with the flesh
on my bones,
while I sing in tones
that I do not know.
OH!
NO!
OH NO!
OH, I AM WHOLE AND FREE
as a lynx or a bee
in a meadow
searching for thee!

NEW MEXICO

THE NEW POLITICS IS HERE.

NO POLITICS!

The public
(John Q. & Mrs.)
is a
Turquoise Lamb
being gnawed by tentacles,
whipped and torn
by the youth
below,
who is a mammal
& a mindless falcon.
WATCH OUT,
Mother,
your plastic tower
has had it
&
is in
disrepair!
TOO LATE to follow up
the empty stair

to nowhere.

AMERICAN AIR

WHY NOT
study the food
as we eat it?
AN INTELLECTIVE
EXPERIENCE.
Scrimshaw of cow
tastes
etched on block of filet.
Black pop-eyes
of shrimp
gone away.
Only the pink body
remains,
made of sunlight
and plankton.
Served with scent of ozone

at 30,000 feet
Loony tunes dancing overhead.

FOR RIP TORN

THE REVOLUTION
is sentiment.
REVOLT
is real.
Instant to instant.
PINK-VIOLET
BARRACUDA
of
SYNAPSE.
Flicker
of meat, sex, death.
ZOMBOIDAL
dunes of bodies drifting.
Ghosts of Condors
plucking the livers
from Giant Ground Sloths
of confusion.

FINALLY

FINALLY WE ARE ALL
HUMAN:
the beautiful girl with blonde
or red mane,
the old man,
the villain, the demon,
the angel feathered
with virtues and loves.
And
we
move
on
the
same
mattress,
DISCOVERING
WE ARE GODS
and finally human—and mammals.

What a lovely foot!

FOR JAMES B. RECTOR

People's Park, May 1969

"This implies that a sulfur atom has specific properties when
it is isolated, others when built into a protein in a solution, and
still others when the protein is arranged in a special way in a
biological structure and is surrounded by a special environment.
Whatever detailed knowledge we possess about the sulfur atom
in isolation, whatever knowledge about the behaviour of other
atoms in the protein (carbon, hydrogen, nitrogen, phosphorus),
we still know only a tiny bit about the potentialities that a sulfur
atom may possess.
FOR EVERY LEVEL OF ORGANIZATION,
MATTER DISPLAYS DIFFERENT PROPERTIES."
AND MATTER IS SPIRIT!
AND MEN, WOMEN, AND BABES ARE
MEAT
SPIRIT
CREATURES
!
AND HELICOPTERS AND TOXINS
ARE LESS ORGANIZED
than the flesh of the earth!
—AND TREES ARE AIR-MEAT SPIRITS.
NEW MEN
are lovers of trees and rivers.
We ARE ONE with the WORMS and BACTERIA,
PANDA, SALMON, EAGLE AND CEDAR.
WE ARE THE BLOSSOM, THE PISTIL,
THE THORN AND THE NERVE.
WE ARE THE SURGE THAT FLOATS IN SPACE,
spores and tendrils of gentle Leviathan.

7

We are the hunters of protein grail,
NUEVO ALCHEMISTS,
man, woman and babe,
deer, bear and virus,
cypress,
worm and bacterium . . .

WISDOM AS SUCH

for Robert Creeley

BE HUNGRY
BITE HARD
CHEW WELL
STAY HUNGRY
HEAD OPEN
eyes
ears
nose
black holes.
KNOW
what you want.
GET IT!

Loneliness is solo
like the empty thoughts from flesh.

SHIVA SPEAKING

MUSK CAVES—body caves dripping like Earth drips meat.
SIXTY MILLION BUFFALO, BILLIONS
OF PASSENGER PIGEONS,
GIANT GROUND SLOTHS,
MOA,
Cave Bear, Kodiak Bear,
GIANT CONDOR,
Woolly Rhinocerous,
IRISH ELK

are

all

eaten!!!

Or killed for the pleasure
OF SEEING DEATH'S FULFILLMENT.

BLANK HOLES,
faintly scented
of musk,

in the Pleistocene we inhabit.
A mountain of wild mustangs turned to dogshit
is studied by ghosts of eagles from the gables
of forests turned to houses and disposable
diapers. Invisible wolves changed to spaces.
Empty cartridge clips and flint chips
buried under concrete
aggregate from ex-river bottoms.

Eidolons of wild berries in rain forests of spirit whales.

UGHHHH!

UGHHHH!

UGHHHHH!!!

SAVE IT!

((Clean up, make new meat waves.))

GOODBYE COUSINS!

Clean it up.

Don't burn it down!

OFF EFFECT

for Sterling Bunnell

THE NET OF DISEMBODIED FACES RISE
LIKE STEAM FROM MEAT.
THEY GRIN AND SIMPER, GROWL AND WHINNY,
WITH EYES AND EARS AND NOSE
and holes that let the spirit in from
THE NOWHERE
they create.
FACES DRIP FACES, and BODIES SPRING
from central source
of protoplasm
that runs amok. (PERFECT PLAN.) A sprawling,
eating, beating, sweet black
FLESH

turned

TO LOVE AND THOUGHT!

BLUEBLACK FLESH NIAGARAS
roar and bellow upward
(as a spore,
or seed,
or a brother's claw or antler)

from a fire
of nerve, muscle,
encapsuled molecule,
atom,

11

FLUNG
to blow itself out
with loving lips,
AND KISS GOODNIGHT,
and stroke its tentacles and wings
IMMORTAL.

Puff!

THE BASIC PARTICLE

WE KNOW OURSELVES
as we swoop to touch
within our aura.
Pseudopods of Messiah
witnessing self
packed in a pelt
—ANGELIC
DEMONIC,
and everything else.
The welts
of Time's whippings
melt away
like August & May.
HERE!
HERE!
HERE!

HERE!
HERE!

MANTRA, BROTHER, MANTRA

IT IS ALL ONE WAR!
SMOTHERED PUFFINS AND AUKS
in crevices.
Oil-soaked cormorants
flopping on beaches.
Seal babes beaten with clubs.
Orientals splashed with
flaming napalm.
MEAT
is
INTELLECTIVE!
Meat is thought!
MEAT IS INTELLECTIVE!

MEAT IS INTELLECTIVE!

MEAT IS INTELLECTIVE!

MEAT IS INTELLECTIVE!

MEAT IS INTELLECTIVE!

MEAT IS INTELLECTIVE!

FEATHER . . .

BEAK . . .

claw . . .

CHARRED FINGER . . .

bloodied fur . . .

13

MEAT IS THOUGHT!

(Herds of Bison the size of poems.)

PLUMES

of the Carolina Parrakeet!

ELF WORDS

ELF WORDS
are great words
too tiny
to be heard
like the whirr of silver
turbojets
within a galaxy.
ELF WORDS
are gentle sweetened
lion roars
OF PLAIN TRUTH
from
a
space
we barely
comprehend.
Kapish?

14

BEGINNING WITH TWO LINES BY EIGNER

the knowledge of death, and now
knowledge of the stars
makes good the gift of gab
they choked us on!!!

THE STARS
ARE
FOR
new gene pools.

FERRETS

MEN

FALCONS

SALMON

born anew

IN NEW SHAPES TOGETHER

NOT, NOT, NOT, NOT,

NOT, NOT, NOT, NOT,

NOT
THE SHUCK
OF WIMPY
ASTRONAUTS.

LET'S HAVE TRUE BEAUTY AND NEW SHAPES
OF MEN!

15

A THOUGHT

flying San Francisco to San Diego

THE MESSIAH IS OUR SHAPES
SPREAD INTO GHOSTS
OF REAL BEING.
We are lumps of beauty upturned
to sense our selves
that spread
from the heads
of our seeing.
Stick arms reaching for axes
chop
the night
we light
with our shoulders touching

to find

((like thoughts in bubbles))

THAT

WE ARE,

WE ARE.

And our surge
may trip
to other stars
that are as we are—
GHOSTS OF REAL BEING
being
real.

NOT YOUTH

Seelge Sehnsucht

IT IS NOT YOUTH THAT INTRIGUES ME
BUT SUPPLENESS.
The sensitivity of meat to meat and to nerve
dies with the nets of self-image.
THE SELF BECOMES RIGID
and does not open
AND EXTEND.
The structure
is frozen and rusts
like armor. Spring comes
and goes
with buds and creatures.

WE LOOK INTO A VISION
and only see
it narrowing. Beyond
that
there is a mystery
in this life like a candle flame
AND

it is moving.

I would be as perfect as a moth.

FRAGMENT

THE BODY IS REAL—HAS DEPTH.
The eye of intuition may see like sonar
all the muscles of the flesh.
And the ear may hear,
like fingers running over crystals,
the hidden meaning
of the words
men speak
to one another. Then
reality in guise of imagination
shows the doors
of new rooms
little known. HOW
BEAUTIFUL THE SUBSTANCE
of them. Like gossamer
preparing for solidity—
or scents of morning
that precede the dawn
within the redwood forest.
—Tiny viny roses
rustle leaves among the roots . . .

THE SKULL

for Charles Olson and Jack Kerouac

WE SHALL BE SWIRLS—SWIRLS—SWIRLS
OF EXPANDING STRUCTURE
and make our New Pleistocene
among the STARS!
WE SHALL BE MEN ((MAMMALS!!))
of infinite beauty!
THE SURGE
will
pour
UNSTOPPABLE.

We shall arise like jeweled
CROWNS
from a hurled stone
in a still pool.

ALL
begins
with OUR protein!
WE ARE THE SUN! WE ARE THE SURFACE
SPREADING,
retopologizing,
SPORING . . .

WE SHALL GROWL—AND WE SHALL SING!!

THE SKULL

ROLLS & COILS AS THE CREATURE

MAN-MAMMAL

UPSTANDS

PARIETAL SWELLS TO FRONT AND BACK
(Occiput accommodates the vision. Dark holes of seeing.)

CORTEX FLOWS BOTH BACKWARD AND UPWARD
TO FIND THE BALANCE

ABOVE PELVIS—HEART—LUNG AND GUT.

The constellative complexities of sensorium

22

SWELL IN A MULTITUDINOUS MIME
OF BEING—SCANNED
BY A SOURCE THAT IS CENTRAL
ONLY TO THE POLYTHEISM

OF SELF

self

     SELF

self

SELF

SELVES MAKING A CONGRESS
OF MEAT-NOTHING

NO SELF LESS URGENT THAN ANOTHER
IN THE CONGRESS.

THE CHAMBERS OF THE EAR ARE THERE
FOR THE SNOW LEOPARD, THE WOLF,
the lichen, and the salmon to speak to.

HE RAISES HIMSELF AND THE BONE
CHAMBER (HOME
OF BEINGS EQUAL TO HEART AND TO GLAND)
WOBBLES AND BALANCES . . .
TURNS SEARCHING

23

FOR FOOD, WARMTH, FRONTIER, SEX, LOVE . . .

is powered
BY THE BULK OF THE MEAT THAT IS
MAMMAL REAL MEMORY AND WEIGHT
AND SOURCE
DERIVED FROM THE INERT SURFACE
ENERGIED BY SUN . . . ENERGIED
BY QUINTILLIONIC GENERATIONS
OF SUN GALAXIES
in past and present future
OF NOW . . .

—IS forever brilliant and unforgetting . . .
knows six billion years of the sculpture
of living surging (ONE CREATURE) plasm
that dances like a sculpture freed
of

TIME   SPACE,

NO
MORE
or less
meaningless or meaningful
THAN A MOLECULE OR BACTERIUM

OR
any facet,
extrusion, or aura
OF THE MEAT

bone   claw   tentacle   fur   tooth   scale   feather
stamen   spore

in the swirl-whirling systemless-system, extending

24

and containing through ellipsis the perceptions and insights
INTO THE IMAGINED INVISIBLE

in which star systems are likewise

PROPORTIONLESS PARTICLES

WHERE

THE BLACK RIVER
becoming Ocean

BREATHE-BEATS
(groomed by seals and sea birds)

IS

sailed by ships and seed fluff
of imaginary physical-molecular
IMAGINATION . . .

does not   dream
BUT KNOWS
in many ways
the laugh, the joy, the screams

OF DRAGONS
dragoning themselves

AND FINDS THE CONFLUENCES THAT BURST

OUT AND JOIN

AGAIN . . . DEVOURS

BECOMES   COUSINS
with all creatures,
jasper, jade, lapis, cellulose, phosphorous,
crystals, fluids. —SYSTEMS INCONCEIVABLE
even to this open system
TOUCH   &   BRUSH
the thorns, velvet, musk,

DIVIDE,
EXTRUDE FROM THE BULK,

REGARD

SELF
(selves)
as tool!
REJECT!   REJECT!
Finds confluence
then
confluence of confluence of confluence . . .
CREATES SHIP OR THISTLEDOWN WITH IMAGE
(condor, atom, galaxy, wolf, cobra, raptor)
on the sails.

SETS OUT

AS (skull) CONFLUENCES (skull) MERGE (skull)

sailing

BA, KA, CHI, PRANA, MEAT, SPIRIT, ODEM.

UPSTANDS   FROM   THE   PRONE   LIMBS
(arm)   (leg)   (toe)   (penis)   (digit)

ALL WAYS
(freed from the instant experience).

Horseback in Libya with Bow. Hunting Old Stone Age by
new star
(covered with fur or not).

PROPORTIONLESS   MELTED
of predisposition
destroyed
(recreated),

MYTHOLOGIES MADE
(instant by instant)
living, sightful, worm-writhing.
THE OLD BRAIN
(in biologic precedence)
balanced against
VISION

VISIONLESS
(as!   !one)

SYMBOL-LESS.
The symbol being

A BLACK DOT

encircled by a band of Halo

27

Held aloft by wings of falcon.
(*pinions*)   (*pinions*)
A dark drop
falls from
the flying globe.
TWO DROPS SPRAY
from the sphere.

Two drops spurt from each drop.
EACH
glistens with radiance.

Smoke spurts from the North of the Globe.

IT IS MIRRORED.

It repeats

finitely   infinitely

(*end of The Skull*)

MAY MORN

TUNING MYSELF BY MORNING COFFEE
—the cup makes steam in the shapes
of goddesses. Molecules
swirl in air. California
edges into sun. Waves lash against
Point Bonita. I sit
—the last Indian—
beating on my drum.
My tee shirt the color
of raspberries—blazoned
with yellow planets.
I am as mad (or sane)
as Shelley
waiting
to be a magian
—resting for action.
AH,
there are doors of tissue gold . . .

PORTRAIT OF A HIPSTER

The eyes are strange—looking out into nowhere.
Behind him
the flag stretches like a sailing ship.
The green stripes smile like Odysseus.
THIS IS BRUTAL MURDER REALITY.
The body is a shield
for what is happening.
Smell of marijuana in the nose.
Scratch of silver on the tooth.
WAITING
to
FIND
SOME BLOODY MEANING!
Grinning and grinning.
Imaginary guns at hip.
Grayhaired quickdraw
artist
be quick!

THRICE BLESSED

HERMES TRISMEGISTUS, LEAD ME
WHERE YOU WOULD—
to Erebus, at the gates of Hades,
where the rigid spiritsouls
dissolve again. Stamp the earth
with your rood, and I will listen.
The glisten
of old scents and memories
is a path for you . . .
Musk, and myrrh, and mold,
and lichen cups of powder green,
arrowhead, and feather,
labor, silence, speech
may be the mother and the father,
matter and the pattern,
of the steppingstones
to you. For what
I see is only fragment,
latticework,
of what surrounds me.
Even knowledge and perception,
side-by-side,
are not enough.
((Huge exemplary visions hang above
our heads, and lie within the earth.))

ON A VISION BY ROBERT DUNCAN

THE RATS IN THE HONEY ARE KINGS
TOMBED IN THE GOLDEN SWEETNESS.
THUNDER CAN RUFFLE THEIR FUR
IN THE LIQUID SUGAR.
Streams of memory flow by with minnows
and water striders at the base
of the mausoleum.
Deer drink there. A bear passes.
Racoons leave footprints
in mud by the watercress.
There are cyclones.
Lightning circles the moon.
The roots of the tomb
reach
into the Paleolithic
and beyond
to join with the single
BEING
and out into stars
and beyond them to nebulae
that vibrate to bees
building honey.

A CELL.

And then another . . . And another.
Of all colors, odors, tastes, touches.

A CELL!

And another. One more! And another!

BEYOND THOUGHT

THE GOPHER SNAKE IN THE CREVICE
IS A GOD.
He raises his head and peers.
He is hungry and mindless.
He is not afraid
only cautious. His muzzle
is smooth and rounded.
The spots and gleams hide him
in darkness where light
breaks against rocks.
There is no reason why a god
must be intelligent.
A god, or a spirit, is free
of proportion—
forgetful and experimental,
does not remember
that I am here,
and slithers to move
into the bright desert sun
by the lakeside, in search of
the mouse
(spirit-god)
who dreams in a burrow, cuddled,
arms drawn tight to his side,
whiskers sleek against his cheeks
waiting for moonlight,
sleep-listening, occasionally trembling.

GRAY FOX AT SOLSTICE

Waves crash and fluff jewel sand
in blackness. Ten feet from his den
the gray fox shits on the cliff edge
enjoying the beat of starlight
on his brow, and ocean
on his eardrums. The yearling
deer watches—trembling.
The fox's garden trails
down the precipice:
ice plant, wild strawberries,
succulents.
Squid eggs
in jelly bags (with moving
embryos) wash up on
the strand.
It is the night of the solstice.
The fox coughs,
"Hahh!"
Kicks his feet—
stretches.
Beautiful claw toes
in purple brodiaea lilies.
He dance-runs through
the Indian paintbrush.
Galaxies in spirals.
Galaxies in balls.
Near stars and white mist swirling.

FROM THE WINDOW
OF THE BEVERLY WILSHIRE HOTEL

THE WOLF'S PROFILE HANGS
OVER THE THREE CROSSES
and is engraved with the letters
of the alphabet.
His eye is an Italian movie.
Drops of blood
flow from the trees.
It is all carved on an onyx
and laid on the grass
surrounded by fluttering flags.

The entire structure
stands on a papier-mâché pedestal
that is cleverly gilded
and antiqued. Its eagle claw
feet are strapped
with black leather
and silver buckles
to the back of a trained turtle
who swims in white steaming chowder
in which float pieces of rainbows,
shards of gold leaf,
and cases of green eye liner.

NEW HOLLYWOOD

THE PARASITIC ANTS MOVE ON THE HUGE
YELLOW BODY
OF HOLLYWOOD (or is it America?).
They have beautiful faces
and sweet intentions of greed,
freedom and power.
The flying bombs nestle
waiting for challenge
of the last nervous straw.
WHILE IN THE FUTURE
dying burning men scream
and claw the flaming air . . .
THE NIGGER GYPSIES
dance and sing
on furniture
that's made
of moving pictures.
Marionettes jerk and sweat
catching kisses from the fans.
Bad men move to worse jobs
like suffering bulldogs
unable to consume enough.
AND IT IS
ALL
O.K.
All o.k.

Living mindless planet skin.
THIS IS WHAT I BREATHE WITHIN.

PARAMORPHOSIS

for Philip Whalen

THE WILD LILACS CREATE FACES
ABOUT THEM. MY HANDS
HAVE PINK AURAS. THERE IS THE SCENT
OF OLD FIRES, MUSK AND BAY
IN THE ROOM. WE ARE OBSESSED
with the War. Nothing else can enter
our senses but the news of death
and destruction. The rooms
of our being are closed. The entrances
BLOCKED

BUT
there is a black fire
in me. With a radiance
of aura above it.
IT SHIMMERS. SECRET
parts of myself
send gyres of energy
to my brow and my eyes project
light in the cave about me.
I
AM
NOT
GUILTY
and now is the time for the pleasure
of exploration.
PURPLE . . . PINK . . . YELLOW . . .
FUR . . . TENTACLE . . .

GLARE

A FIRE

PERFUMED SMOKE

Feathers and wings sprout from my head.

Hooves from my fingers.

FACE

**THE WILD LILACS STAND IN FRONT
OF NASTURTIUMS.**
A yellow face floats over them.
The face is outlined by pink.
There is a scent of bay and musk
and old fires. There
are flashes in the air
of silver gray, scarlet, and blue
that represent
the patterns on the sidewalk
as I pace
pulling
it
all
together.

99 THESES

1. MAN IS A CARNIVORE EXPERIENCING HIMSELF.
2. MAN IS A MAMMAL.
3. THE UNIVERSE IS THE MESSIAH.
4. THE CREATURE IS ONE BEING.
5. ONE BEING IS POLYTHEISM.
6. THE 27 SENSES ARE EXTRUSIONS OF MESSIAH.
7. THE SENSES ARE GODS AND GODDESSES.
8. THE MAMMAL & THE STAR ARE EQUAL.
9. THE STARS ARE A GAS.
10. THE GALAXIES ARE A LIQUID.
11. ALL LIFE IS A MEAT SCULPTURE FREED OF TIME, SPACE & DIMENSION.
12. THIS SOCIETY IS A CAGE FOR THE MAMMAL.
13. ALL CREATURES OF WING, FIN, FUR, TENTACLE, PROTOPLASM—ARE EQUAL.
14. THE PANDA IS A PEACOCK.
15. MAN IS A PANDA.
16. THE SALMON IS A MAN.
17. THE WOLF SINGS.
18. CARBON, HYDROGEN, NITROGEN, OXYGEN, SULFUR.
19. THE STAR IS A SUN.
20. CHILDREN ARE FREE.
21. THE BODY IS A CHILD.
22. THEISM REJECTS THE MESSIAH.
23. THE PHYSIOLOGICAL BODY IS PURE SPIRIT.
24. EACH SELF IS MANY SELVES.

25. THE INVISIBLE EXTENSIONS OUTWARD ARE AS COMPLEX AS THE VISIBLE EXTENSIONS INWARD.

26. THE SENSORIUM, MEMORIES, AND GENES—ARE CONSTELLATIONS.

27. ALL CONSTELLATIONS ARE ONE CONSTELLATION.

28. LIFE SURGES.

29. EXTINCTION IS AN APPEARANCE.

30. THE SNOW LEOPARD IS A WORM ELF.

31. EARTH IS A SNOW LEOPARD.

32. LIFE IS TOPOLOGICAL COMPLEXITY.

33. WEALTH IS ENERGY.

34. ELECTRONICS DEVOLVE FROM THIS STAR.

35. THERE IS NOT INTELLIGENCE BUT INTELLIGENCES.

36. CRUELTY, TORTURE, SELFISHNESS, VANITY— ARE BORING.

37. EACH MAMMAL DESERVES.

38. THE SLOTH AND THE EAGLE ARE EQUAL—MEN ARE EQUAL IN THE SAME WAY.

39. THERE ARE, AND ARE NOT, MOLECULES AND ATOMS.

40. ONLY THE SELVES CAN DOMESTICATE THE SELF-DOMESTICATED.

41. MAN AND THE DOG ARE SELF-DOMESTICATED.

42. MEN FEED WILD MUSTANGS TO DOGS, AND WHALES TO CATS.

43. THE SEA URCHIN IS A GREAT PHILOSOPHER.

44. PLATO EQUALS CHARLIE CHAPLIN—JESUS IS ANACREON.

45. MONEY IS FUNNY.

46. THE DOLLAR IS A COLLAR.

47. CLOVER IS A CREATURE.

48. THERE IS ENOUGH WATER FOR ALL WHO SHOULD BE.

49. EVERYTHING IS NATURAL.

50. REASON IS BEAUTY.

51. MEAT IS THOUGHT.

52. THE GREEKS WERE THE LAST TO DEIFY THE SENSES.

53. MONOTONY IS MADNESS.

54. THE FRONTIER IS OUTSIDE.

55. THE FRONTIER IS INSIDE.

56. LIFE BEGINS WITH COILING—MOLECULES & NEBULAE.

57. RELIGION, MATERIALISM, POLITICS, PROGRESS, TECHNOLOGY—ARE EVANGELISMS.

58. EVANGELISMS ARE PROLIFERATIONS OF MONOTONY.

59. REVOLUTION IS SENTIMENT.

60. REVOLT IS BIOLOGICAL.

61. THE LIGHT ON YOUR FINGERTIPS IS STARLIGHT.

62. PROPORTION AS MEASUREMENT IS FALSITY.

63. THE BLACK MAN IS NOT THE PINK MAN OR THE YELLOW—THEY ARE MAMMALS.

64. DREAD THE POLITICO AND PREACHER WHO CAN DELINEATE A MESSIAH.

65. NATIONS ARE FALSE DIVISIONS OF CONTINENTS.

66. CITIES ARE SWIRLS OF POPULATION.

67. IT IS NATURAL TO DROWN IN CITIES—IT IS NATURAL TO SWIM IN WAVES.

68. THERE IS ONE LANGUAGE—GESTURE, VOICE AND VIBRATION OF BODY.

69. YOUTH IS CLUBBED WHEN IT RISES OR OPENS.

70. THE BODY IS ELF LAND.

71. THE CHILD IS A BEAST OF BURDEN—HE IS USED FOR WAR.

72. LIFE IS NOT REST BUT ACTION.

73. LIGHT AND DARKNESS ARE ARBITRARY DIVISIONS.

74. THE FIST IS REAL—THE MACHINE GUN, BOMB, NAPALM, ARE FANTASIES OF COMMUNICATION.

75. PROPAGANDA IS NARCOSIS.

76. POPULATION IS AN ADDICTION.

77. LOVE CAN ONLY BE MADE, OR INVENTED, WITH MEAT.

78. PRISONS AND COURTROOMS ARE MONOTONY.

79. WAR IS ONE COLOR.

80. THE PUSSY WILLOW, THE REDWOOD, THE BUTTERFLY—ARE BLOSSOMS.

81. MADNESS IS TEMPORARY AND NATURAL.

82. WHERE THE BODY IS—THERE ARE ALL THINGS.

83. SOUL IS BORING—SPIRIT FLIES.

84. THE CRICKET IS A WARRIOR AND A GOD OF MUSIC.

85. THE FALCON IS A CLOSE AND TEMPORARY ACQUAINTANCE.

86. ANY SEXUAL GROUP IS APPARENTLY NATURAL.

87. CLEANLINESS IS UNDEFINABLE AND AS NATURAL AS FILTH.

88. DRUGS ARE BRIEF ALCHEMY.

89. MORALE IS VIGOR.

90. THE YOUNG CREATURE IS AGILE.

91. THE OLDER CREATURE IS STRONG.

92. WISDOM, MEMORY, IMAGINATION, ARE SEN-SORY CONSTELLATIONS OF INTELLECTIVE MEAT.

93. MODERATION DERIVES FROM MULTIPLICITY OF EXPERIENCE.

94. NOW SUCKS.

95. PAST, PRESENT, FUTURE AND DIMENSIONS—ARE A FIELD FOR BALANCE.

96. LUCK IS A CREATION OF THE MEAT.

97. LUCK AND MEAT ARE DIVINE.

98. THE EYE AND TONGUE ARE A FIELD OF CREA-TURES.

99. MEAT IS A MOVING CAVE IN THE SOLID AIR.

—Paris

APRÈS ACID

AHHHHHH, THIS IS HEAVEN WHEN I AM
A BLACK FIGURE AND WE

ARE IN ETERNITY!
The wind blows the fleece.

WHITE FUR IN THE BREEZE
AND SCENTS OF MUSK.

Camping out in always as we always do
I see that you and I are free.
The ceiling is brown with age
and there are words upon the walls.
Auras come and go about our heads
and we reject them
for our freedom.
The fire cracks and snaps.
CAMPING
OUT
ALL
WAYS
in radiant eternity.

WE ARE FREE!

In the darkness of a dignity.

FREE CREATURES 1.

THE EUCALYPTUSES CREAK IN THE WIND
—branch against branch,
trunk rubbing trunk.
WATER
drips
cold and wet
to the earth below.
The scent dances in the forest
in wafts and tendrils
among the blackberries.
Fuchsias explode
scarlet and white
in the twilight.
You stand on tiptoe
picking leaves
for our rooms
this first day
of September.
I
KNOW
THAT
WE
ARE
FREE
BLACK MONUMENTS
TO
A
FIERY
SPIRIT.

THERE IS A NEW PLATEAU OF BEING!

A BREAKTHROUGH!

I HAVE SEEN IT!

GRAY DARKNESS IS AN OLD MYSTERY
to be cracked.

WE ARE FREE CREATURES!

FREE CREATURES 2.

THE DARK BUSHES OF ROSEMARY
are a mystery. The purple blossoms
are eyes seeing into twilight.
The sprigs bring
in fog
from the peaks.
MY EYES
OF BODY
reach into spaces
I cannot see.
I reject
the auras of rebirth
and the spirit diving eternally
to look into the fire and space
and
be
a
free mammal.
FOREVER!
A
TRILLION
SENSES
LIBERATE
me.

Agnosia!
Tenebrous cloud
lit by our passing.

WITH TENDRILS OF POEMS

WITH TENDRILS OF POEMS,
WITH PERCEPTIONS
LIKE AMINO ACIDS,
the gray plateau is eaten away
and becomes humus for the senses
to feel. Space
is created in the solid dullness.
Scents appear.

Beauteous mephitic odors from green flowers.
Dust in the beard.
Art Nouveau butterflies.
Cliffs shaggy with gardens.
Marble.
Pearls.
Lilies.
Jade.
Song sparrows. Flames.
And the WHOLE BEAST self
laughing and slouching and striding.
SEPTEMBER BLACKBERRIES!

BEGINNING WITH WORDS BY P.A.M. DIRAC

". . . it is more important to have beauty
in one's equations
than to have them fit experiment."
YEAH!
YES!
—And the figures fly
through us with smiling faces
and eyes alight
but sometimes we delight
in denigrating them.
The radiant trails of their auras
and secret senses!
The body can only be diagrammed
with bright colors,
intense odors,
streams,
stars,
and constellations.

OCTOBER FIFTH

BEAUTIFUL FLESH-COLORED DAHLIAS
IN THE MORNING!
JANIS JOPLIN IS GONE!
Today is the festival of Departed Ancestors.
You were the coruscating star.
Big Brother danced like mad geniuses,
electronic Rimbauds,
and Amerindians. Then,

like everyone else, you became mad
with
arrogance.

What do we have but that?
And song so meaningless it is
silence.
The delicate fruit we eat
is the food of war
—AS
YOUR
SPIRIT
IS.
It is all O.K. now
where you are.

THE MEDIA AGAIN

THE PSYCHOPATHS SHOW US OLD MEN
and young boys and say
they are surrendered guerrillas.
The elders are skeletons!
What could keep them
in the jungles
so long
before giving up?

Liberty?
Mao?
The bald eagle?

Twist stomach.

BY THE FOREST

YOUR EYES TELL ME TO QUIETLY
TURN MY HEAD.
—There is a hummingbird
hanging midair, mindless, intent,
bulging black eyes,
glistening green,
protein-electric
—sipping nectar
from the bouquet of fuchsias
spraying
in my hand.
HE IS
MECHANIZED
MEAT
IN
FLUSH
of full spirit.
—All speed and solid muscle!

MOTTLED SKY BLUE

THE BOUGHS, THE LEAVES, differentiate space.
How different in the vase
than at the forest.
The change is merest
transformation by mammal hand
but now they flare in new proportion.

When the eye goes wide
and high and all about,
the ego flies
—anagogic.
The temple draws
me out
within its bounds.
But the peak and copse
transpose
all I am and know.
I am freed of the social layer.
I
fly
with the little hawk.

NOTES ON YOUR DREAM

BLUE-PURPLE BLOSSOMS OF WILD LILAC
scattered on gleaming wood.
LUCENT YELLOW PETALS OF DAHLIA
on dark earth.
QUASARS VIBRATING
in space.
WHITE NIGHTGOWN
embroidered with red roses,
the softness of your face,
and the bed we lie upon
ARE
ALL
I'll ever know.

—And those other waves of matter
that we find our love within:
dreams, bodies, babes,
horned horses,
and wild rides.

TUBBS ISLAND

for Gary Snyder

THE TUFTS ON THE BANK SLIP BACK
TO THE SALT MARSH.
The waves eat beneath them. They fall.
The tides make new shapes.
Proteins, sugars, and nitrates return.
The sparrows sing like Shakespeares.
The osprey dives
making a splash.
As lassos in a rodeo,
the glides of raptors
overloop:
marsh hawk, sparrow hawk,
white-tailed kite.
Shorebirds
blow and settle like gravel
and probe for the carnivore
whelks and worms.
Tendrils of orange dodder
twine on the pickleweed
drinking out nutriments
to create
bitty white blossoms.
Look, there
is
Mount Tam—and MOUNT DIABLO!

FATHER

NEITHER AM I TROUBLED IN HEART
nor am I afraid.
Countless have gone before me
preparing a place—or no place.
The wall is old masonry
—beautiful and crumbled.
The sky is blue
in front of the darkness
and there is a rainbow
and stars in the day.

Hail, strange man
WITH
LIGHT
STREAMING
TO YOUR BROW!

ODE TO JOY

I HAVE INHERITED THE UNIVERSE!
IT CAME FROM THE EARTH
that got it from bodies
that became divine.
Ocean, forest, fog,
are wine
and they drink me.
Nothing bad
can ever happen
—it is part of the constellation
—part of the code.
It is all an ode
written in eagles
and plasm.
The chasm is as drunk
as the dizzy height.
What joy to be in flight.

TWO DRUNK POEMS

1.

I LIVE IN ETERNITY

IF I SPEAK ABSTRACTLY
MY BRAIN IS AN OPERA
OF OLD AND NEW MUSIC
taking the shapes
of another century
AND
YOU
WILL
HEAR IT
VERY CLEARLY
a
million
years
in the past
or the future.
Mammal. Animal. Death.
Love. Intellect. Reason.
Madness. Beauty. Hatred. A trillion
faces shine around each word
with lines beaming from them.
And you will hear it very clearly.

2.

MY FATHER IS A BABE
AND AN OLD WOLF;
the gulf between us is sealed.
The field
is eternal and inviolate.
We are one!
WE ARE ONE!
WE ARE ONE
and the rattlesnake grasses
sing his praise
in the days
when heaven is unfolded
AND
I
AM
FOREVER
A
POET!

APPARENT SENSE

IT IS APPARENTLY IMPOSSIBLE THAT WE CAN
ANY LONGER ACCEPT that thing which we have been
trained to recognize as the universe. We can believe that our
five senses are true to us. But it is the US that has been altered.
Why are we not wolves? Why are we not wolves as much as men
and women? We feel the howls and loves in ourselves. We know
that we are part of the same sculpture of plasm. WE HAVE
KNOWN THIS FOR SO LONG THAT I AM CRAZY WITH
LOVE.
AND I HOLD IT WITHIN ME
LIKE A BOUND DOVE.
That we are so much more than we dream!
I am a stream
that joins the river
of all that we are.
The stars reflect in their own gleam
AND
WE
ARE
FLOATING
FREE
IN
THE MOUNTAIN OF MEAT AND AIR.
Oh, who are we that we do not care
but stare and do not feel
the pealings of ourselves as we flare
mortal and immortal?
The faces we know are eyeless Xes
with flames and rainbows above.
WE LIVE IN ROOMS
within our teeth,

and speeches that we make
are free.

GONE ARE THE NETS OF PROPORTION.

Away with the walls of fact.

MOIRÉ

for Francis Crick

1. THE CHANTING IN TIBET HAS NOT CEASED—IT IS AS IMMORTAL AS MEAT.
2. HORNS, CYMBALS, AND LIGHTNING BOLTS OVER GLACIERS.
3. BEARDED SEA OTTERS CRACKING MUSSELS ON STONES ON THEIR STOMACHS.
4. COYOTES LAUGH AND PRANCE ON POINT REYES.
5. REVIVE THE PLEISTOCENE.
6. PLEISTOCENE IS NOT GLACIO-THERMAL—IT IS MEAT-MAMMALIAN.
7. CRACKS IN THE SIDEWALK REFLECT THE DISPERSION OF CLOUDS AND AURAS OF COLOR.
8. REALITY IS A POINT, A PLATEAU, A MYSTERY.
9. IT MAY BE PENETRATED.
10. WILDFLOWERS: MAN ROOT, SEPTEMBER BLACKBERRIES, MONKEYFLOWERS.
11. POEMS AND PERCEPTIONS PENETRATE THE PLATEAU.
12. SUCCULENT GARDENS HANG ON CLIFFS.
13. THE VELVET BUTTERFLY AND THE SMILING WEASEL.
14. BENIGN VISAGES FLOATING IN AIR.
15. SPIRIT IS ACTION.
16. ACTION IS PROTEIN.
17. BONES OF THE SABER TUSK IN ASPHALT.
18. MOTILE POEMS LIKE FINGERS OR ROOT TIPS.
19. AMINO TRIGGERS IN SPACE.

20. WE ARE ACTIVITY.

21. BELOW US IS STEADY AND SOLID.

22. SOON ENOUGH.

23. PERHAPS WE RETURN TO A POOL—STEADY AND SOLID.

24. NO MATTER—ANTI-MATTER.

25. WE HAVE THE JOY OF HERETICS.

26. WE DID NOT CHOOSE IT—WE ARE.

27. PERFECT.

28. PERFECT PLATEAU BECOMING ODORS AND TOUCHES.

29. I DID NOT KNOW THIS IS NATURE.

30. THE BLANKET FLOWS OUT OF THE WINDOW— ON IT ARE YELLOW BANDS WOVEN WITH RED BISON.

31. SOLID BLACKNESS ABOVE AND BELOW.

32. MUSIC BETWEEN.

33. FORESTS OF MOSS IN THE COLD STREAM.

34. BULK OF A DEAD SEA LION—DARK EYES OPEN.

35. THE DESERT IS ALIVE.

36. THE FIR FEELS THE SOLSTICE.

37. SENSE HORIZONTALLY, ASPIRE VERTICALLY— *AGNOSIA*.

38. KEATS, DIRAC, DIONYSIUS THE AREOPAGITE.

39. TRUMPETS, CYMBALS, WARM GRASS, ROAR OF A MOTORCYCLE.

40. LEATHER, QUARTZ, AND CINNAMON.

41. DISSOLUTION IS A PRIVILEGE.

42. HAIL PLANARIAN!

43. SWEET, WARM AND ODOROUS IN THE AUTUMN SUN.

44. BLACKER THAN BLACK, BLUE-BLACK—A MIRROR REFLECTING REDS.

45. SCREAMS AND FLAMES OVER THE HORIZON.

46. CREAK OF EUCALYPTUS BOUGHS.

47. THE PLATEAU IS A POINT, THE MASK OF A DIMENSION.

48. THE MASK IS ENFORCED BY ENSOCIALIZATION OF PERCEPTIONS.

49. SEPTEMBER BLACKBERRIES ARE FREE.

50. THERE ARE STILL BLOSSOMS.

51. CONDENSATION FALLS PATTERING ON LEAVES.

52. MACHINE GUNS COMMUNICATE BULLETS.

53. BOMBS ARE SYMBOLS FOR MEAT THOUGHTS.

54. FACES OF MALEVOLENCE AND FOLLY STARE FROM THE WALLS.

55. THE FLEECE MOVING IN THE BREEZE BY THE FIRE IS LOVELY.

56. WE ARE OLD WOLVES, INDIANS, CREATURES.

57. ETERNITY BECOMES BROWN-GOLD FOR AN INSTANT.

58. TIME IS THE LONG WAY BACK.

59. IGNORANCE, LIKE INFORMATION, IS A LEVER.

60. THE BODY'S ODORS—THE BERRY'S ODORS.

61. THE MASS OF INFORMATION WHITES OUT.

62. RAINBOW AGAINST WHITE—PROJECTED ON BLACK.

63. THE SELVES FLYING THROUGH THE BODY HAVE FACES.

64. THEY STREAM WITH TAILS OF COLORS.

65. SENSATION MAY PRECEDE INFORMATION.

66. WE DIVE BOTH DOWN AND OUTWARD.

67. SOLIDITY AND VIBRATION.

68. UNEXPECTED PROFILES AND FACES.
69. THE BRAMBLE TANGLE IS A MOVING SCULP-TURE.
70. DRAGONS OF SPACE AND MATTER.
71. FALSE PERCEPTIONS MIMIC THE REAL—A COVER.
72. THE BODY MAY BE DIAGRAMMED WITH COL-ORS AND ODORS.
73. THERE IS A FIRE AND TRAJECTORIES OF ENER-GIES.
74. BEYOND THE MASK OF THE POINT ARE TRIL-LIONIC INTERLOCKED CONSTELLATIONS.
75. PLEASURES ARE NOT RELATIVE BUT ACTUAL—BLACKBERRIES, SEA LIONS, TENDRILS.
76. PERCEPTIONS ARE HERETIC—THEY NEGATE ABSENCE.
77. ABSENCE IS LACK OF PERCEPTION.
78. THE MUSSEL SHELL CRACKS ON THE ROCK.
79. WAVES OF WATER AND PROTOPLASM.
80. COYOTE SHIT—THE TAJ MAHAL.
81. WINGED TIGERS ENCASED IN TRANSPARENT SILVER.
82. MY WHISKERS—THE WOLF'S BEARD.

(end)

SPRINGS

1. I REMIND MYSELF THAT THE UNIVERSE I HAVE INHERITED IS DIVINE.
2. FACES DIVINE AND TWISTED.
3. STILL DIVINE.
4. VOICES SNEERING AND ARROGANT.
5. STILL DIVINE.
6. DISSOLVING CITIES—DIVINE.
7. FOX SPARROW, JUNCO, CANNIBAL SALAMANDER UNDER THE LEAVES—DIVINE.
8. PRESENCES OF ALL EXTINCT CREATURES—DIVINE.
9. THE ONE BODY OF ALL—OF WHICH I AM A FACE OR FINGER—DIVINE.
10. THE HEAD OF A WOLF PRESSES OUTWARD FROM THE ENDOPLASMIC RETICULUM OF A PHAGOCYTE, AND HOWLS AND SINGS.
11. A RAINBOW GLISTENS OVER THE SINGING WOLF HEAD.
12. DARK SHAPE-CREATURES FLOAT—MOVING—OVER THE RAINBOW.
13. SILVER GALAXIES FORM OVER THE SHAPE-CREATURES.
14. THE GALAXIES DRAW TOGETHER TO CREATE A PHAGOCYTE.
15. PINK PLUM PETALS FALL TO THE TABLE TOP.
16. LEAVES CURL DAY BY DAY.
17. SHAPE-CREATURES APPEAR IN THE VASE.
18. A BLUE VELVET NOTEBOOK AGAINST SLICK YELLOW CARDBOARD.

19. NOVALIS FLYING THROUGH SPACE WITH MADAME CURIE.
20. THE MYSTERY OF PORCHES AND DOORWAYS.
21. THE BLACK PERCEPTIONS OF CHILDHOOD DRAWING INTO A BALL IN THE OLD MAN.
22. FEARS CHANGED INTO LOVES—LOVES CHANGED INTO FEARS.
23. PIANOS—EXPLOSIVES—CAVERNS OF CRYSTAL.
24. MY DEAD FATHER WITH THE SMILE OF HIS BABY PICTURES.
25. EXHAUSTS OF AUTOMOBILES—DRAGON VAPORS FROM HOLES IN STEEL PLATES IN THE STREET.
26. DREAMS OF BABIES CREATING UNIVERSES.
27. THE ERODED BANK FALLING BACK INTO THE SALT MARSH.
28. PANDAS CHEWING BAMBOO SHOOTS IN CHINA.
29. THE UNKNOWN SUBSTITUTE FOR THE LUMINIFEROUS ETHER.
30. SHADOWS IN THE DESERT.
31. SHADE IN THE FOREST.
32. THE ODORS OF VENICE.
33. THE HARBOR OF HONG KONG—CHICKEN SHIT AND PERFUMES.
34. THE PLEASURE OF TRUTH.
35. THE FREE CONSTELLATIVE PATTERNS OF THE BODY.
36. CAVES OF BROKEN CONCRETE.
37. NEW MOSS.
38. THE CUPS OF LICHENS—A POOL FOR THE CONJUNCTION OF ALGAE AND FUNGI.
39. WARM SUNLIGHT—SWALLOWS SINGING BEFORE DAWN.

40. THE AGONY OF EXISTENCE IS DIVINE—SO IS
    THE PLEASURE.
41. WATERFALLS OF SOFT FUR.
42. SPRINGS OF COLORS INTERMIXING IN THE
    MEADOW.

A THOUGHT ON POINT REYES

MOUTHLESS AS A MAYFLY
with moons on my wings
of red, brown, yellow,
gold,
I
play
for a day
and then fly away
like raspberries in December.

XES—A SPONTANEOUS POEM

I am one with the euglena, triceratops, mammoth and sea urchin. I am one with the universe of matter and energy as well as the fields that I do not know of consciously or verbally. All these are contained within myself. My self, or selves, is a part of all. The surge may be inter-universal—may drift through all time and space. I am an extrusion, a tentacle, a point, a pip, upon or within this happening.

Yet I am no more or less important than the whole. Politics and social strata are a natural projection (among many possible projections) of my closest of all cousins. They tell me that I am a man. I know that I am a mammal and part of ALL. I want cousinship and I write rapidly and without judgment to make an artifact that is less and less a part of the social strata of Man. I wish to make a poem that is an act of nature—more free of the conditioning that I call politics.

YES CHRIST
LET ME BE COUSIN TO THE *BEAST* CHRIST

I KNOW I AM!!!!
ARMS EXPLODING AND TENDRILS FLOWING.

((MESSIAH, TATHAGATA—MAMMAL-ME!))

Extrusion of the instant experiencing myselves
—acting from the coiling in myself, creating—
and seeing all faces, visages, and fingers
in the air.

NOW
I
AM ME
WHEN I AM ALL!!!

Cousinship to rock and crystal but
mostly animal. MAMMAL LIKE A PLANT
IS *LIVE*.

UNTRAMMELED BY THE NAME OF *MAN*
and free!
Liberty to make myself with warm-blood style—
and unconditioned.
Attrition
is a growing Surge!

THAT COLD MOUNTAIN
is a vibratory aura-statue
of
WARM FLESH!

THAT *IS* POLITICS

73

HAIL THEE WHO ART THEE-THOU-ME!
SPENGLER AND THE PANDA!
Instant life adrift in Space. Wolves and shepherds,
elk, and parsley in our cells. The brains of being
shaping outward then encurling. The Other
Universe o'er which we flit like ether-gnats
in trembling squadrons
on the mountain air.
FOR I AM MAMMAL, BEAST, CREATURE!
NOT
a Man!

((Not invented THING but ME! I am
the Universe!))

The Universe that trembles on the Other solid Thing.
—And I am glad and battle here
with my conditioning
with
THIS
and
THAT
and stinking glimmering
glittering flittering hammering
images of lies
that bring no skies
into my consciousness! ! !

HAIL THEE
(wherever)
for we are free
to be
a cousin or a sister or a brother!

HAIL THEE WHO ART ME BURNING
BLOSSOMING TRANSMUTING
changing matter to complexity becoming timeless
in the Change. Holding back the Pain and grinning,
laughing, eating, loving. Making emphasis
in novelty of self that is a dimple or a wing.
Pseudopods stretched out to see the Other Selves
of ONE. BUT NOT THIS ONE
we see. All Ones. On this PLATEAU
we make, invent, and ARE.

NOT THIS SOCIAL THING!
This mean conditioning!

PRAISE
TO THIS POINT
we are and feel.

Praise to the Pouring through all the webs
and chambers. Flow to the Flow. Implosion
and fissioning into the spiral that whirling,
coruscating outward goes. Joy to the poor
mammal wit that sees the pleasure of it!
System of Systems
BECOMING
((All ways—All times))
creature-creatures

OF
ONE

BLOOMING THING

75

YEAH, YES, AND NO PAIN, NO PAIN,
BUT MAMMAL STYLE
AND SHAPE AND EVEN GRACE. Free to know (BE)
a Quasar, cyclone, foot of forest floor, ring
of Saturn, flatworm, philosopher, free atoms
drawn to solid heavy space again.
And oh so easy in the choice, it happens
in the Luck.
NO CHAINS! NO ARMOR
except for decoration in divine.
The Choice to swing a saber—make a kiss.
FIND
A
MAMMAL CODE
((Freed of Good and Evil!))

Cool or warm—full or empty.
Inventing virtues
—diving through the fogs of fear!

The Selves that grew from One find one
MEAT INTELLECTIVITY
inseparable
from self-contained and probing

TOUCH! ! !

LET ME DRAW TOGETHER IN THE FULLNESS

AND I REACH TO TOUCH THE LUCK!!! NUMB
DUMB, GLEAMING GLOWING
—SEEING RAINBOWS
IN THE SNOWING OF ALL LIFE
through Space. Touching. Breathing. Parting.
Setting style from inward shape of meat
till
flesh is shapely style that smells
and eats itself. Existent
in the Now and Past and future.
Particulate. Accruing. Reassembled
in the living Plow.

But clearly—freed of mind—whirling, sensing,
knowing All. Not tortured. Not pained! Smiling,
expanding, OR being ALL at *any* point. PLATEAU

FOR
VISTAS

OF
THE

infinite senses

BEING BAGS OF DUMB DARK MEAT KNOWING
ALL PAST PLATOS!
FEELING-BEING BEAT BY WAVES!
ROCKED ON GRAVEL.
COLD OR WARM—indifferent. THE SPACE ABOUT

a cave of knowing.
Pouring eggs and sperm from long-forgotten triggers amplified.
Ideal forms—a merry laugh. Existent-not.
Or not-existent. A flitting daydream of reticulums.
Pointed. Dull. Smooth. Full. Scraping. Hungry.
LOOPING TO
long-haired Men
writing documents

with quills of birds

to scratch abysms

DESTROYING ACTING
stratifying, inventing searching senses,
becoming as always
STARS, BAGS, MAMMALS, EUGLENAS
—ONCE AGAIN

TELLING US (ME-THEE),
"JOY"
of it.
((Dead word!))

IT
IS
ALL
RIGHT
PERFECT! GROWING PERFECT ALL WAYS!!!!!

AND RE-ENTERING BEING, NOT BECOMING
—BUT ALL WAYS.
Always Expanding contracting. THERE ALWAYS
in any instant or century or evolution
to simplicity or complexity. Lord Byrons.
Penguins. Gingkos. Herds of bison roaring and flames

of prairie grass afire. Stars dancing like
a sect of sperm cells worshiping themselves
in accoutrement of goddess. All action
or stillness. Plumed hands reaching
through holes to scribble
on the scrolls in strange chambers.
Sought
and
unsought—all the same.   (! ! !)

((POLITICS? HAH! THEE-THOU-ME.))

DREAM DIVING AND SWIRL-FLYING AS IF
THE BODY WERE ELECTRON MICROSCOPE.
Selves grumbling in their congress. Grottoes made anew
in constellations. Flying Tigers strafing
troops. Topology of flakes of snow. Body
banners furling, fluttering, in the fields of sense!
Recognition to recognition,
FLASHING THROUGH THE NET!

Winking and devouring—divine complicity.
All at Once!
With past and future
flayed and drawn and quartered,
mysterious,
fresh,
falling all around the mammal
toying in the shapes
upon the edge and in the center.
Enlayered, folded, laid to rest
like fields of groundflowers
blossoming in rain.
And fingers from the stars that touch their brain
of self

FOX SKIN ROUND MY NECK
—TALON ON THE DOOR!

DRAMA?
Why not be merry tortured, self-loving!
What have I but me and all? A mammal
powerpack not even split away.
FINGER
of all my reaching
in and out and every other
DIRECTION,
way, path, past, door.
Energy entertaining self to glorify the universe!
Longing. Hoping.
SEARCHING FOR THE SOLID
STUFF I'M MELTED IN
AND AM.
To stand at edge of tundra, truck, auto. Occupying spore.
Not split off
but intermingling.
Singling
incidents to cluster
selves about—as if

I choose

YOU DO

I DO

We are . . .

AND EVERYTHING: EACH TITMOUSE,
SPARROW, PHILOSOPHY,

OR VERB. Free to fly unbounded. Fall drifting
in banks, be shoveled, pressed against, compressed,

chiseled, laughed at, sculpted, invented,
imagined, dreamed, tossed in streams

FLOWING
all around one
(creature)
like the forest plasm sent out
(and rippling through)
exploring in counter-reflections, refractions

NOT
being by chance
of particles, and laws (for real) or
no laws

BUT BREATHING
as we know we do
and being meat in it
from the inside outward,
rolling on the floor and growling by
the pretty feet

KNOWING EACH POINT MERE PLATEAU
OF INFINITE IMPORTANCE!
New Year's Day—Birth of Universe.
Duckling in the egg—split of amoeba—
point of light in salmon's eye, Nova.
Free and interlocked. Rocked
in the knowledge of a mammal's arms.
BABES
leaping at each instant as always.
Water mold upon the stump of quince stem.
Leaves unfold
—and blossoming each day.

Praying for the powerpack
to break the shackles of domesticity

WHEN
IT
IS DONE,
THERE, NOW, FREE, ALWAYS AT THE TOUCH! !

ALL AROUND!
Not beckoning! ! ! !
Caring or not uncaring total life!

THE LUMPEN SHAPES RISE UP—PRESS
OUT—LIKE BOYGS
with fang and claw and gun and club and wing.
With halos overhead or gleaming

figure eights that boomerang and dance
from one to other to flitter overhead.
And all dissolves, drips down, to be the edge
of vision like a pair of lips, a chin,
A BROW.
And another tiny figure rises up
in fresh alarm. Visages reverse.
And smoke and flames arise from
BURNING BONES.

OR CALL IT ANY THING!
THE RUG DESIGNED WITH NEITHER BIRD
NOR FLOWER
afluttering. Wave intermingled
with wave upon the edge. Turquoise
streams pouring into yellow marshes
intermingling

mangled by design.

BUT meat-knowing presses through

making mammal sight

to see

an unsought daily vision

SMELLING SONGS OF BIRDS.

GRAINS OF WOOD CARRIED IN THE BLOOD,
AND ODOR-ALTARS
BURIED IN THE CORNER OF A ROOM.
Meat-manuals stacked high—outshielding,
pushing through conditioning.
Politics adrift within the air and poking
IN
with dull and stupid
manic eye.

PRAISE TO THE GLORY OF THE BEAST! ! ! !
THAT HE *IS* BEAST!
And Flesh!
ASTRIDE (and in) THE SURFBOARD
of the Universe!
Smashed quicksilver whirling
on a polished floor!
Breathless games
sans rules!

(*SECRETLY*)

FIRE SIRENS, SIGHS, SWEATS OF JOY
AND PAIN. THE VAIN
SIGHT OF SELF, SEEING,
THE ULTIMATE GLORY!
(((Complete
destruction
of philosophy!
SELF-LOVE INVENTING LOVE
FOR REAL.
THE FEEL
OF MEAT.
THROUGH KNOWN AND NOT.

)))

Not melting, not dying.
But clearing plasm—fearing not.
Being free to fly through all. No shout
to cheer or call. Self-willed! The wills
OF SELVES
appropriate experience. ONE FLESH
SNOWS
through Space
and catches into solid holes . . .
Diamonds, carbon, leaves, and cooled energy
that mimes resurgent past and future . . .

Ambitious as a fir.
SWEARING
BY
NOUGHT
and
NOTHING
SAVE
THY SELVES! ! ! !
LAMB'S DREAMS CAST AWAY—OR SAVED
in precious boxes.

86

ROLLING CRESTS OF EVERGREEN IN
MINIATURE. SPONGES. FURS
of wolves with Chinese moons. Nectar hungers
in the brains of moths. Meteors with mirror-image
aminos bringing fresh news in form or shape
of actions. Potentialities full blown
to be puffed again.

HUNG IN TIMES AND LEVELS! . . .
NO SUCH THING! NOT EVER
Never
Any Place!
Imagination freed of all image
but the latent possibility. The news
SPREADS
making selves that know by pressures,
movements, motions. Shambling
on the edge and burning in the center.
Turned inside out, and then en-writhed,
wreathed, spansuled, uncapsuled . . .

WHILE SHACKLES STRANGLE
IN THE SOCIAL STRATA!

I
am one. /
You are another. (Shit!)

Ensocialized?—Or MAMMAL!

AND I REACH TO TOUCH THE LUCK! ! !
(SECRETLY.) OPEN.
Ephemera—like all. Beauteous. Curious.
No Good nor Evil. Glowing pressure.
"Holy?" "Sacred?" SOMETHING ELSE!
Scent of sulfur? MASTODON?—OR STAR?
Divine Trash billowing
like clouds my flite dives through
AND IS.
Lamb, Man, Dog—boxed out—and IN!
Conditioned
in the Surge.
Simplicity become complexity as poison.
DEAF!
DUMB!
BLIND
—to nets of shooting stars!

(*finis?*)

BEGIN!
To know the feeling-being Vibes. Star dots
darting through the interwoven fields.

AND HAND, PAW, CLAW, CILIA, PLUME
—REACHES THROUGH
and scratches on the nothingness that floats
upon the edge. Makes facing features, shapes,
bumps, contrives itself, invents the images
it is. Throws out. Draws together.
POURS. Giggles. Roars. Particles
lay down layers projected from the parts
of selves. Entrapped. Free like
thistledown in cyclones . . .

SOCIAL STRATA — YOU AND ME

Thee-Thou-Me is better.
Warmer.
Fuller.

WE

SHARE

ONE THING! ! ! !
With sea cucumber, panda, plasm . . .

(Un-named—Un-nameable.)

SEPARATIONS ARE APPARENT . . . COUSIN,
BROTHER, SISTER.
All one starry thing of selves and selves
of selves of selves of selves of selves of selves
like interiors of stars before the
cooling. Like wet galaxies
in tissues pouring waterfalls
of living glimmering
sparkling metals. So slow.
A flash to infinite senses. Here.
Thee. There. Gone Forever. Now.
AND
OLD
VIRTUES
PISSED AND GONE!

Why woe? Why sadness? Why
CONDITIONING?

This is (WE ARE) nature!

(BOXED?)
Yeah,
but free in being—being free
in liberty past liberty. SEE IT!
A pink petal crushed in hand . . .
Darkness is a newborn gland . . .

BEGIN

THE CARVING OF THE LATHES, PLASTER,
MEAT, ENVIRONMENT,
flying ships, and fantasies, and spores
that close or open doors
of flesh-thought that mimics
in material the consternation
of a part of us.
Drop behind the darbies, links,
and locks! Set up the Sight
that starts within.
Set in from the outside. Smiling.
Snarling. Tear up, shape-out,

take
potentiality
as loops immersed in futures
canceled or made more free

TO BE

AND SEE

AND BRUSH AGAINST   !

Why not? Oh, speckled, smirking, glowing,
AURIANT GLORY
that we
sculptured ourselves!

(for Jackson Pollock)

PLUCK OUT MYCELIA OF SOCIAL PERSONALITY
FROM MAMMAL-STYLE.
Neolithic acts in mime of torture.
Turning, twisting, very fast. Pain
distorts from pain, Politics
is doomed and meat is free
to feel soft pleasures,
beams,
scents,
tastes,
and inheritance of self
from selves. The intersections

of the memory are points. A NET. Within—forgotten things.
Points are lids. What we see—is real. What we know—con-
ditioning. We beg for art and get a net not bio-nature.
Plead for science—receive measurement. Not meat-science!
Ask for vision?

Here's a lovely Social Tract! THOU HAST KNOWN IT ALL
BEFORE!
NO DOUBT!
Sensory starvation!
STAND UP!
Being-Liberty! ! ! ! !

VEILS ADRIFT WE SLIP WITHIN
—UNKNOWING.
GRUNTS HURLING FRAG GRENADES. Monk
tranked at his piano.
Dreamers in the painted caves.
GALAXIES ON WALLS. CREATURES
IN THE EYELID.

BINS OF MONEY, OBJECTS,
PLASTICS ARE NO ACCOLADE!
Nor rest, nor sleep, nor ease!
The fork,
the new path,
is back
at the barbarous
DISTORTIONS.

THOU KNOWEST
NO MACHINE

can do this. No

program

no
new knowledge
in the timeless

SLIPPING . . .

DREAMING . . .

POURING . . .

EYE . . .

HOLE . . . NODE . . . CURL . . . COIL . . .

UNWINDING . . . REACHING THROUGH
TO BE THYSELVES . . .

REACHING THROUGH TO KNOW THY ELVES . . .

EXPANDING . . .

BILLOWING . . .

Cousin, Sister, Brother . . .

(*End of Xes*)

SLICKS

Where it washes on tidal rocks at Bolinas the oil from the tanker collision is one to three inches thick. It's like the skin of a leprous vampire elephant, gray-black with brownish iridescence. Cormorants, grebes and ducks flopping in it become more and more mired. The cormorants are covered with a quarter inch of the bulk oil—only their scarlet glittering eyes are clear.

1.

THE SKIN OF A VAMPIRE ELEPHANT
(like the daydream of a general)
gray-black and wrinkled
—brownishly iridescent—
washes
back and forth
between tidal rocks.
CORMORANTS,
GREBES,
DUCKS,
strangle, choke,
smother,
caught
in
produce of ancient fern forests
puked out by a rammed tanker.
Scarlet eyes of dying birds!
Thank you, Standard Oil!
Bless you,
Ghouls of Congress.
Death to whales, seals, sea lions
standing between us and victory
in Vietnam!

95

Praise
those who rubberstamp murder
in Occupied America.
IF
ONLY ONE
MONSTER
WOULD DIE WITH EACH BIRD
IT WOULD SEEM WORTHWHILE!!!!!!

2.

WHEN THE MAMMAL WITHIN REGAINS
CONTROL OF MAN, REMEMBER
TO TRY LYNDON JOHNSON, KENNEDY,
LAIRD, ROOSEVELT,
McGEORGE BUNDY, AND EVERY
CONGRESSMAN, AND SENATOR
for genocide. For the Jews, Poles, Vietnamese,
the mountain gorilla, the red wolf,
the grizzly, the Indian, the Blacks, the tiger,
the whales, the rhino, the polar bear,
the flightless parrot,

and for the extinction
of the intellectivity
OF
ALL
LIVING CHILDREN!!!

3.

ENOUGH SAYING, AND HEARING, THAT
WE ARE ALL PRODUCTS
OF OUR TIMES AND THAT NO ONE
IS RESPONSIBLE.
It's time to jail the mad who are powerful
and make harmless the mad who are indifferent
to their madness and to rapine, murder,
and destruction. It is time to clear out
Occupied America. The sneaky process
of Junta
is more than thirty years old!
Each bite
of delicate food
and
each film entertainment

IS
THE
GIFT OF WAR!

We are not products.

TATHAGATA VALENTINE

YEAH, YEAH, YES, THUS MOVING
SMASHED AND BILLOWING.
CONTRITE AND SNARLING-SMILING. FLEEING
forward through conditioning
of fogs. Tissue vapors engulf inert.

ORGANS

PUSSY WILLOW POLLEN

DIVING
on the selves
enmeshed and outward pouring.
Tasting touching time.

Yeah,

yeah,

yes,

CLAW

FEATHER

MULTICOLORED SKINS.

The huge machinery of freckles
and of grins.

OVER THE LEFT SHOULDER, MR.

for Dennis Hopper

THE BLUE-BLACK CLOUD COVERS THE CHIN
—A SPARKLING GREEN AURA SHOOTS
from the head. There is the smell
of civet and roses. I fill
with esthetic pleasure. THE WAR
takes place somewhere over
the left shoulder.
Happens some place
several thousand miles
away . . .

((((THERE IS A CLOUD OF A MILLION
DEAD ASIANS—BUT
it is over the left shoulder
as
somewhere near my feet psychopathic
killers high on acid—like
a cancer in eternity—kill
a pregnant movie star. SCREAMS,
PLEADINGS, SHRIEKS,
GIANT
FIGURES,
tiny like memories of this
instant . . .))))

and
we
smile
speaking
of the future
and of hope. WE

ARE HOPE FULL!

99

THE GLOW

THE GLOW OF PEARLY PRIDE
IS SELF-ENJOYMENT
—reveling in bare arms
moving water,
or the growling
heard as speech.

And the elf within
and the gorilla,
they know
there is pleasure in social sin
and the love of self
and the secret grin
and the slender finger
silently swirled
in the scented world.

SHAKESPEARE'S BIRTHDAY

SHAKESPEARE, WITH YOUR ANGRY MICE
AND LAUGHING SPIDERS,
HUMAN FALCONS, GENTLE LOVERS
wove in nets
of bodies
striding, singing, plotting, praying,
spitting, kissing. (HOW
THEY MAKE A WATERFALL
or fountain or cascade of blossoms
or a sugared or envenomed
torrent.)
Now
we
watch
you once again
as ever. Sniffing,
listening in the dew-swept
fields. The fox,
the hedgehog, roebuck,
and the pride of princes
roar around your luminescent brow.

All
the pains of politics and meat
give birth to more than Art.

CARVED ON A BOX

IT IS THE CLOSENESS OF PERSON TO PERSON
that makes the split
on a diagonal
and draws up the mouth
in one-sided sneer
CREATING
&
PEELING BACK
the mask
to show
the flowered fang.
Ah, yes!
Oh VILE!

POEM WRITTEN LAST NIGHT IN THE MARGIN

SINCE LIGHT EXPLODED
from my eye
I
touch
the beams.
SEEING-BLINDNESS.
All
one
thing.
A
cactus-
daisy
of
deigned
delight.
Life
rains
in
all
directions.

Soft grass.

Echinoderm.

Blue-green algae.

Marten.

MARGIN POEM

DOT BLURS OF MEANING AND SENSATION
—WE ARE—
among quasars
and
galaxies.
Points
of
pain
and
pleasure.
Whiting-
out
to
the
nodes
of
meat.
Quicker
than
a
feedback system!
Aristophanes
knew it!

FOR JANE

THE YOUNG LADY CAT (TIGER TABBY)
sits, paws folded
under breast,
on green grass
in the cool
summer morning
haze
listening
to
families
of
pigeons
and
a
Vivaldi
concerto.
Very
pleased
to
be.

MUSTARD

LUCIFER'S FATHER WAS AN ANGEL
(at the very least).
The dark heads
of sedges
are signatures
between the blades
against
the drifting sand.
The rites
of creeping buttercups
enact
themselves.
Pools of milk
and galaxies
entwine.
Moth's feet
grasp
owl's
down.
Bouquets
gestate
in mausoleums.
Boulders sleep
by
motels.

A SPIRIT OF MOUNT TAMALPAIS

DEER BONES AND FOX SCATS
dry in the late
spring sun
watched over
by
yellow mule-ears
and blue-eyed grass.
Buckwheat   Cries
Brodiaea   of hummingbirds
Bunch grass   in
A vulture (close)   the
Bee plant   wind
Crab spider   on
Garter snake   the path
Seaside daisy   through
Grindelia   the chaparral.
Coyote bush   Bright
Poison oak   vision
Cow parsnip   light.
Wild iris   Ocean
Baeria   below.
Buttercup   Hello,
                          Lew!

MILLICOMA FOREST

IF COLETTE
is fields of wheat
and Baudelaire
is an ancient African lake
then
I must be
Michael
McClure.

_____

Azure claw.

- -

Three cooper hawks cry
—aharrying.
The babe learns
to dive
on prey.
We
lie naked in the sun
on tables.

GATHERING DRIFTWOOD ON
CHRISTMAS MORNING

1.

OLD APPLES FROM DARK SWANS
DROP IN MY HEART.
NO!
Not "Heart"
but
SOUL
—or say "Spirit"
as spirit is glassy peaks
of living foam reflecting waves
upon wet sand on Christmas Day.
From above stare down steep hills with veins
of serpentine and chaparral slowly roaring
toward the sea.
And we are ONE and ALL—held together
by
this fantasy
of sun and grin and meatly
molecules.
And it riffles slightly at the edges
like a calm but smirking
almost merry dream.

2.

"My senses fail / burning fires devour me,"
goes the song.
BUT
here is the foot of a gull
held in my hand in the cold air.
Gray soft bumpy
webs
between three toes.
LIKE SILK!
And here's
the body of a grebe
BULBOUS,
with long thin neck and tiny head
with pointed beak
all made for diving, lying flat
upon the strand.
I hold it up laughing
gassed with wonder.
You'll
remember.

FROM THE BOOK OF JOANNA

JOANNA, YOU'RE BAD! YES,
YOU'RE ROMANCE!
I won't pat your arm again BUT
I'll remember all the pain
and beauty
that we've known together.
How your body is a little girl's.
FACE
WITH
WRINKLES
that
I've
grown with—and I love.
And yes, they're sexual—
as you are and
you know.
Sure
we've ripped at each other.
We've invented ugly little Hells.
(Though I'd rather be in one with you
than in Heaven with another.)
We've made some Heavens too, like wafting
feathers in the pillow or the air beside
the fire—or on a balcony in Paris—
or a sportscar in the desert underneath the moon
—or swimming in an icy ocean like we come together.
AND
I'VE
HEARD
YOU SHOUT
SO OFTEN
with sexuality
in full pleasure! ! !

111

(Do you remember? Sure
getting old is getting
old. WE'VE
GOT
FAR
TO
GO

and you're still so BLACK.

I love your toes and breasts

and butt and shoulders

and your winsome smile and all

the trails and veils of romance floating from you

when you walk.

FOR
YOU
ARE

MY

QUEEN
OF PLEASURE

and
if there's darkness in me
then your demon reflects it back

TO SOMETIMES MAKE AN ANGEL

112

and sometimes make a blessing in the guise

of fangy wolf

FOR

only you

can sometimes

let me know SHEER LOVELINESS

and only I can be your dark and fumbling guide

TRIP

Faces on a Greyhound bus.
Tracks of beetles
in the desert
dunes.
Trees all made
of green thorns.
Shards of pottery
in ancient lava
mixed
with bones
of antelope.
Baby
bunnies
held
in
arms.
Worshiping the light
of reason
after endless
pain.
My star magnificent
slipping into morning.

FROM A MAUVE NOTEBOOK

WE ARE A CHILD WITHIN AN AGING CAGE.
BUT THIS CAGE
has wings
and radiance glowing
from each soft and scented feather.
Whirlwinds of arms
sprout from the wicker bars
and it all
stands on tiptoe
leaning
toward the stars
and throwing kisses.
Laughing.
Snorting
like
a
lark.
Unafraid of dark.

SONG WITHIN A SONG

OH, WE ARE LOVELY CATERPILLARS
in the ugly rose.
This hand
this nose
sometimes
stare out and make
a black and merry song:

"The time is long
when we dissect
the universal whale
but
like
little elves
in
Paradise
we
cannot
fail . . .
we
cannot
fail . . ."

Ah, here is my cocoon
with yellow scallops
on the edges!

THE MAGIC THEATER

for John Lion

THEATER DUST ON MY BOOTS
like radiant elf chalk,
I
stamp
around
at night
behind
the
scenes
and grin.
Listening to whispers
and to cries.
Wings upon my brow
—and staring eyes.
Watching creatures dance
in silhouette.
Explosions.
Tears.
Tanktreads.
Bites
and
veils.
(All real
or not,
I cannot
know.)
Even footlights
make new trails.
The air is filled
with booming whales.

Actors grow bright
golden scales
and coil
their stingered tails
as they fire
their souls
through the space
from stage
to
mind.

NINETEEN SEVENTY-TWO

SO, AT LAST YOUR PERSONALITY
HAS BECOME A COPROLITE!
((Fossilized shit!))
HOW
painful it was
to grow up in the fifties!
WE LEARNED:
materialism,
macho-competition,
greed.
BUT STILL I CAN HARDLY BELIEVE
that you sit there telling me:
about the girls you fuck,
how much money you make,
and of your fame.
As if
the last twenty years
never happened.

You
seem pathetically
foolish.
But there is viciousness
in
our generation.
YOU
ARE
REALLY
SET
(like a robot)
ON OVERKILL.

119

And you believe
in social appearances.

You want to be like
The Big Boys.
Whoever *they* are!

AFFECT

THE ASSAULTS YOU MAKE UPON MY MIND
WITH MIDNITE FOLLIES
are
IMPOSSIBLE.
Withdrawal of feeling is an act
(a real gesture
not just a simple hole
in space.)
When you suck
back love
then
REALITY ACHES ME,
and we
sit in
a stupid
HELL
like puffs
of plastic.
We are acrid
and painful
to our senses.

BUT
there is a world out there
with cherry blossoms in fog
and beautiful Chinese horses.

A LITTLE TIBETAN POEM

EGO OBSESSIONS DRY UP THE BRAIN
TO SCULPTURES
of
revenge-acts
and then reverberate
(to tear the beautiful arms
to aching bones).
I
SAY
I
AM
A
LOVELY
LOVELY
LOVELY
MOUNTAIN
IN THE RAIN
with cool waterfalls
and scents of fir trees
round my ears.
I laugh high above the plain.
Little clouds are drifting by my nose.

JOANNA'S NEW POEM

LET ME BE ELASTIC, OPEN ALWAYS
to new change,
a flange,
that turns either way
upon
a shaft of light
of clearest meat
and purest poetry.
Let me be oxen sleeping in the snow,
or a giraffe held at bay
by wombats
on an ice-cream island,
or a soft gray
pussy willow
scented with the morning
dripping rain,
or a panda
pondering on the thoughts
of newts adrift
in copulation
floating past rusty cans
in sunny streams.

WRITTEN AFTER FINDING
A DOLPHIN'S SKULL

YEAH, OR MAYBE LIVE IN FANTASIES
WITHIN A DOLPHIN'S SKULL!
I
can
hold
it in my hand!
I can look in through
the foramen magnum. SEE
the huge chamber where
the lovely creature lived
in part (where
information organized).
SEE THE BLOWHOLES WHERE THE BREATH
passed through and made
a faint cloud above warm
waves.
OR
IT
IS
POSSIBLE
to
cast
around
the Pleistocene
and see real mammal creatures
in the last nooks and crannies. THE EXPLOSION
IS ALREADY HAPPENING!
WE ARE IN THE MIDDLE
of it! It is different! It is not a flare
of three seconds that envelops all
and leaves cinders. It expands
exponentially—in the use

124

of energy. And we
can't see it. BUT
LIFE
IS
BEING ROLLED
BACK WITH A ROAR
and it is best to think the war
IS LOST
and we are survivors
of the Future.

OUR EYES AND EARS AND NOSE ARE DOTS
of intelligence!

IN TRUTH, WE ARE ELVES AND FAIRIES
leaving luminous trails in air like
antlered giraffes,
hairy mammoths,
ground sloths,
giant lemurs, otters, shrews, mice,
cloud tigers, dermoptera, the shi,
badger people dancing with the coyotes,
fox spirits, star-nosed moles, giant pandas . . .

ALL!
ALL! ALL!
BRIGHT AND REAL
hovering over scented beds,
locked in meatly pleasure:

125

ONCE!

EVER!

NOW!

IT IS ALL THE SAME!

At precious moments!

WHEN WE ARE THREE D SCREENS
OF ACTUALITY

adrift in actuality—adrift and living.

Loving being real and free . . .

Lit like flying turquoises driving through the flesh
of time

BAJA—OUTSIDE MEXICALI

AMERICANS PASS BY,
WORLD LORDS,
hauling huge land vans
and campers behind
trucks pulling
dune buggies and power boats
of hallucination.
Great timid Gypsy Lords
of plastic objects
and shining metals
roar at 85 miles per—
out of their secret
walled strongholds
in Orange County
where safe
from commy Blacks
and Chicanos
they pile up
mickey mouse
treasure.
They tear on by
the now dry desert
delta of the Colorado River
—which was polished
off by Boulder Dam
and all her babies
to make power
and give water to thirsty
Los Angeles.
Mexico was paid off
with a diddy bop
irrigation project
and a market for cheap
agriculture.

The Rio Colorado
power is and was used
to build the art-
ifacts on wheels
that thunder by.
Mexicans watch
from dust drenched adobe
under palm thatch
or sometimes
from
a purple and yellow house
and they envy.
The wind-moved tamarisk
trees are beautiful
as graygreen chinchilla fur.

WE

a poem of the bio-alchemical war

1.

SURE, YES
WE
CAN
LET INTELLIGENCE FLOW
AND THEN WE'LL BE SOMEWHERE ELSE!
That's the trick! We'll come home
from the wars with bloody dirty fingers
and our minds on fire
WITH FEARS
of what we've seen.

WE TELL OURSELVES THAT WE CAN
CHANGE THE SCENE!

AND SURE IT CHANGES (to be our nerve's shape).

We can build bombs
in basements and have visions like Boehme's.
Pray to be Blake when Blake's
proudly presented in every bookstore.
We can imagine Gryphons drawing carts with spinning
technicolor bodies for their wheels.
BUT
STILL
WE
STAND
HERE
WITH
MEAT
AT
THE
BOTTOM
OF
EACH
FOOT,

131

GRINNING IN THE SUNSET,

UNLESS WE KNOW THAT SOMEWHERE

IN SOME BLACK SMOKE

NOBILITY IS FIRE!

AND
SPIRIT IS A DEMON
scenting odors in the Surge it drives.

2.

SURE! IT'S NOT SOLVED THERE.
Not where THERE is.
NOR IS *THERE* A SOLUTION SOMEWHERE
ELSE.
There's not a place for
such things.
Unless in dreams.
It's not easy because we
DIDN'T
ask to be here
or for beauty. THEY
were
not
put on us. We
are shapes that fill
a pattern that moves here where
we have come to move—and we know

132

it—and strangely it hurts us to know
such things. 'It is not fair,' we say when
we see it in childhood sitting on an apple bough
and looking deep behind our eyes.

But five segments conjoin
to make the heads of insects.
THE JELLYFISH (THE MAN-OF-WAR)
IS A COLONY
of creatures. And we
accept such things. We see
strange beauty that
THEY MAKE

WE MAKE

FEEL HUGE QUAVERING CLOUDS MOVING
AT THE SPEED OF LIGHT

3.

. . . AND THEY'RE THE SIZE THAT WE ARE.
We know electricity
in the rabbit's touch. Hug
the bunny—feel electrons flow
like fields at the base
of a lover's
spine
—power in flesh relaxing.
REVOLUTION, CONQUEST, PHILOSOPHY

133

will not blow the psyche up
will not bring us
back to touch
or wake
the dead
from vales
they're
dancing
in!
Maybe VISION will
if vision is style and more.
If style is acts we know
we make / in perpetuity.
When we do not join
the dancing guzzling dead
slurping blood and mouching

WHEN
WE

KNOW CLEARLY

BEYOND THE LAUGH OR CRY

—AND CRYING, LAUGHING

touch a cloudy tree of spines
at the duney desert edge—walking

toward the river

and read the book of creatures' feet in dust.

4.

Then we know flat calm felty velvety
loveliness can flow
and blow
itself up
TO BE MORE.
WE HOPE FOR IT.
BUT
FINALLY
THIS   IS   US
and we ARE our Souls
or Spirits—or what
you will.
Like Dante, we're really
down to it!
THIS IS OUR DARK WOOD, OUR LEOPARD,
LION, WOLF.
Our reflection bouncing off any cloud is the only Virgil.
Beatrice is our senses running wild
not some lovely lady
conversing with heavenly Rachel
in moody moony beams.
WE'RE REAL.

and there may

OR

MAY
NOT

be a nanosecond's pleasure!

THIS IS US
and here we stand

135

like comedies
and tragedies
locked in one
Pirate's
chest of treasure

slithering

gritting teeth

smiling like a baby angel at delight in taste or sound

5.

THE HORMONES, AMINOS, POLYMERS DRIPPING
IN OUR BODIES MAKE GREAT MOVIES. WE'RE
HYPNOTIZED
by
esthetics.
'BUT
THEY
are
not really
US!
NOT REALLY,' we say!
We're sure that we're somewhere else watching.
We know the falcon stooping happened long ago.
THE FLIGHTS OF SOULS ARE DIVING
THROUGH THE BASEMENT DOOR

UPWARD TO FLITTER OUT LIKE MOTES
OF SILVER DUST IN BLACK
SUNBEAMS. THE UNIVERSE HAS FLIPPED
WHILE WE LIE UPON
OUR SHEETS AND GOBBLE BONBONS
WITH THE MORNING NEWS!

Yeah!

WOW!

(wow????)

It's all O.K.

NO
IT
IS NOT!

BUT

WE ARE TRYING!

AND THAT IS LOVE!

(Not some airy shape that hurls a kiss at us . . .)

6.

AND

WHAT   A   KISS   IT   WAS   !!!!!

WE MADE A STATUE OF IT.
Beautiful like a Doric Aphrodite turned to softened air
in pentelic marble. A nude kiss with hints
of the discrete. BUT WE WERE BOTHERED
by the sounds we heard. There was
something in the air that clattered
like a billion antlered rattles.

AND I KNEW THAT YOU KNEW
THAT IT WAS ME!
AND
we
landed

there.
Running fingers through
the long green moss, smelling
sedgy flowerets. Watching
wars of beetles
in the waveless water.
Discussing all immortal shapes.
UNABLE
to put a palm
upon ourselves. Forgetting
suns
are stars. Acting

out the real with paperclips

and chalk and butcher's twine,
old egg cartons and trained
slugs
(waving eye stalks)
taking
the parts of tigers.

SOMEWHERE (YES SOMEWHERE) RADIOS
WERE GRINDING OUT

UNDREAMED MESSAGES THAT DID NOT
equal
our discussions!

We were shadowed by the statue!

7.

SO YOU GOT THAT STRANGE GUN
AND KILLED THEM.
And here we are!
(Most of them died in flame and poison.)
AND
THAT
IS
SURELY
FREEDOM.
SO
the Way Out is to do it
once again and hope for better luck.
Perpetuate the reflection of delusions!

Sticks laid crosswise make the fire
—AFLAME!

139

We tamp the powder in the tissue, then the pipe,
and take timed fuse or beauteous bacteria
bred to be pure poison
or
light waves
guided
into shrieking fire
and
DREAM
THAT
PHILOSOPHY
FREES
US.
Strolling in the strange dark forest.
Stumbling over heaps of cones.
Hearing auto horns and fairy choruses . . .

8.

PINE NEEDLES BREAK THE SUNNY
SKY TO PRISMS
· IN PATCHES
when we're in darkness looking out.
Red fungi peep through detritus on the forest floor.
Helicopters clatter in the air.
I or YOU or WE dive out—circling.
The sun beats on waves. Whales grin
in sleep. The city sighs through
a million breaths. Muscles ache
and honey pours. Boats come aground
on beaches.
Trucks crash.
Ice cream melts. Trillionic

140

particles collide
in smaze. And
YOU (or I) loop about
being
FALCON,
BAT,
or
BUTTERFLY
or
lost elfin cherub hoping for a dream
and pouring sweat of fear that damps
even our poor flame!

KNOWING THAT WE SHALL WHIRL AND CRASH
AND FALL PROSTRATE

but open, even then, like a daisy
on a pillow.

OUT

DARK

ARISE!

BE
NEW

BEGIN

BUT KNOWING

WE MUST START

141

9.

AND *AHHHH*   HERE IS THE BLACKNESS!
HERE I AM!

HERE I AM! AND   *AHHHH*
HERE IS THE BLACKNESS!

HOW GOOD TO HUG MY KNEES
and dive rolling while the sten guns
clatter overhead and dirt makes ripples
to the side where metal rips up roots.
OR
TO
BE
OLD
when pictures fall away within the brain!
THAT'S LIVING BLACKNESS TOO BUT NOT
THE KIND I MEAN!
I mean the kind we whirl around in—before
we even touch the earth.
(AND WE TOUCH IT TO BE REBORN
OR PASS OR BE THE SAME
AS EVER ONCE AGAIN)

I MEAN DOWN HERE IN THE DARKNESS
WHERE WE'RE THINKING, THOUGHTLESS!
BLACK STARS. TENEBROUS APPLES.
GLYPTODONS OF INK THAT FLOW.
Dark sparklers in the shadows of invisible Fourth
of Julys beneath black walnut trees beside the mausoleums
flowing away
from us in rivulets
of all that's dull or ugly.

FOR THEY ARE ONLY SO AS THEY ARE LAID
ON US—THEY'RE OUR
LIVES
and not
our plights.

AND PERHAPS I WILL ARISE

I WILL ARISE

I WILL ARISE AS YOU

I WILL ARISE AS YOUR PROUD MAMMAL

I WILL ARISE

I WILL ARISE

I WILL ARISE

I WILL

AND HOLD OUT—GLISTENING ON MY HAND
—WHAT IS PURE AND FREE!

(end of WE)

PUCK

THE SERIOUSNESS OF ANIMALS
IS
MONUMENTAL!
The absolute intention of the snake fly
and the bee and the tiny creatures
that zoom in the sun
among pine boughs. And the arthropods
mating! Even the play of the rats
and the rabbits is serious.
What a perfect world!
Without entry or escape!
EVEN
where the

MEAT-WE

splits
into two
branches—even though
we look across at insects
from a fork
a billion years
cleft away
in evolution
IT

IS

ALL

THIS

SERIOUS

WORLD

—and to be carefree
is to be a soft and laughing star.

INDEX
OF TITLES
AND FIRST LINES

148